HUMPTY DUMPTY'S BEDTIME STORIES

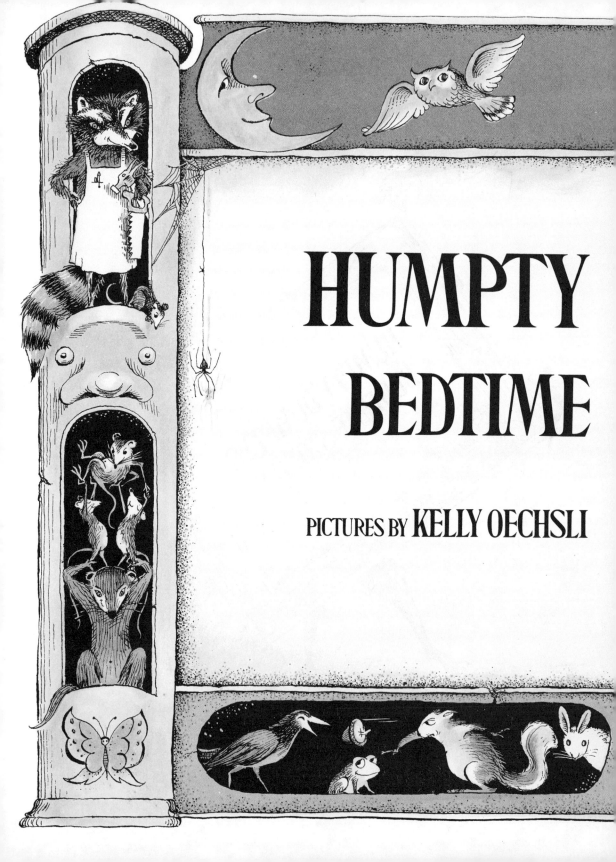

HUMPTY
BEDTIME

PICTURES BY KELLY OECHSLI

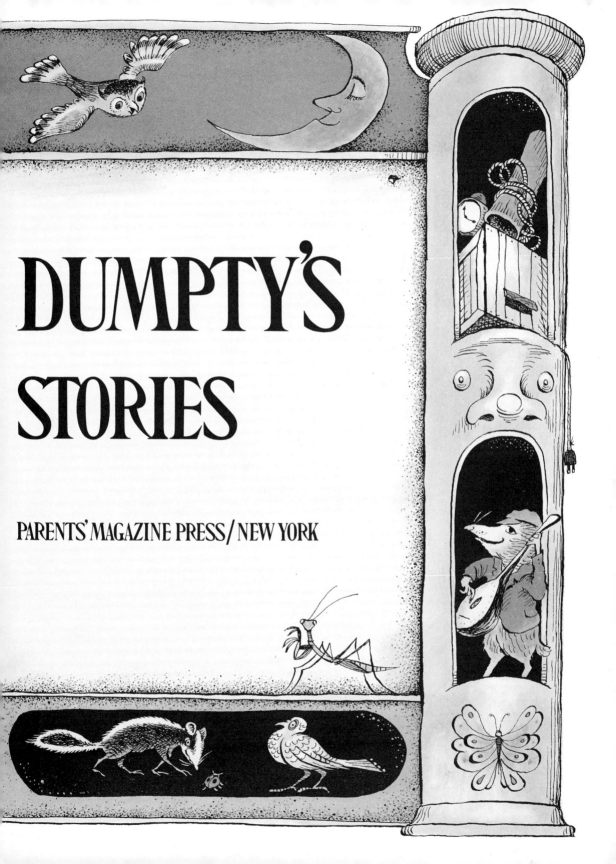

DUMPTY'S STORIES

PARENTS' MAGAZINE PRESS / NEW YORK

Library of Congress Catalog Card Number: 79-136997
ISBN: Trade 0-8193-0502-2, Library 0-8193-0503-0

CONTENTS

THE PATCHWORK PUPPY

BY LILIAN MOORE

Once there was a puppy who did not look like a puppy at all.

He was not brown.

He was not gray with white spots.

He was not a black puppy, or even a white puppy with a black tail.

No, he did not look like a puppy at all.

And that was because he looked—of all things—like a *patchwork quilt!*

He looked just like a grandmother's quilt!

The little dog did not mind at all that he looked like a patchwork quilt.

He thought it was a most interesting way to look.

But there was something he did mind very much.

It was all right to *look* like a patchwork quilt. But it was not all right when everyone thought you *were* a quilt.

Indeed not!

The Patchwork Puppy lived in the woods. He was very happy there. But he did not get much sleep in that woods!

Once he found a good place to sleep under a big tree.

Just as he closed his eyes, something woke him up. A little gray squirrel was trying to squeeze in under the puppy.

"Whatever are you doing?" asked the puppy crossly.

The little squirrel jumped back in surprise. "Oh!

I'm sorry!" said the squirrel. "I thought you were a patchwork quilt. I always did want to sleep under a patchwork quilt."

And away ran the squirrel.

"Silly squirrel!" said the puppy.

Another time, the little dog found a good place to sleep by the brook.

Just as he closed his eyes, something woke him. A little brown rabbit was trying to squeeze in under the puppy.

"What do you want?" asked the puppy.

The little rabbit jumped in surprise.

"Oh! I'm sorry!" said the rabbit. "I thought you were a patchwork quilt. I always did want to sleep under a patchwork quilt."

And away ran the rabbit.

"Silly rabbit!" said the puppy.

The next time it was a skunk.

Then it was a woodchuck.

"Oh, dear!" said the poor patchwork puppy. "Every silly little animal in the woods wants to sleep under a patchwork quilt. I must find another place to live."

So the little dog ran out of the woods to find another home.

He went on and on till he came to a farm. He looked around.

"This is a good place," he said. "Now I can get some sleep."

The little dog found a good place to sleep. He lay down and closed his eyes.

He was just having a good dream about a big

bone, when something woke him.

Two yellow baby ducks were trying to squeeze under the puppy.

"Go away!" said the puppy crossly.

The two little yellow ducks jumped back in surprise.

"Quack, quack!" said one duck to the other. "He's not a patchwork quilt!"

"Quack, quack!" said the other duck. And away they went.

"This is no place for me!" said the Patchwork Puppy, and off he went again.

He went on and on until he came to a pretty green field.

He looked around.

"This is a good place," he said. "Now I can get some sleep."

He lay down and closed his eyes.

All at once something woke him. He looked down.

There, right under him, he saw—not one mouse —not two—but a whole family of little gray mice!

"Oh, no!" cried the little dog. He jumped and ran off.

He ran and ran until he came to a town.

But he was so sleepy now that he could not go on any more.

He was so sleepy that he stopped right outside a little red house and went to sleep.

A little girl lived in the red house.

Her name was Ellen Victoria.

When she came out to play, she saw the little dog sleeping right outside.

"A patchwork dog!" said Ellen Victoria. "Isn't that nice! Just like the quilt on my bed."

She picked up the sleepy little dog.

"I know just the place for you to sleep," she told him. "Right on top of the patchwork quilt on my bed.

"Right next to me.

"That's the best place for a patchwork puppy to sleep, you know."

And it was!

TIMOTHY'S TREE

BY GAIL STEPHENSON

In Timothy's yard stood a maple tree.

Robins built nests in it. Fat, gray squirrels scampered through it. And Timothy's gray kitten climbed it. But not Timothy. Timothy couldn't.

Timothy tried, but the maple was too big, and Timothy was too small.

He tried to shinny up the tree, but the trunk was too big around. Timothy reached—he stretched—on tiptoe, to touch the first branch, but it was too high.

Timothy jumped—time after time—trying to grab the first branch. And he almost could—almost but not quite.

"If I had a ladder," said Timothy, "THEN I COULD!"

"No," said his mother.

"Or a stool, or a box, or even a boost," said Timothy. "THEN I could climb the tree."

"No!" said his mother. "Not until you're big enough, all by yourself. Then you may climb the tree."

And Timothy asked, "When will THAT be?"

"Someday," said his mother.

"After a while, before long."

"How?" asked Timothy. "How do I grow?"

"You eat and sleep and play," said his mother. "And little by little, every day, you grow bigger and bigger and bigger."

So Timothy ate and slept and played, and went on growing bigger.

And the days went by and he kept on trying to climb the maple tree. But he didn't grow bigger fast enough.

So Timothy found a little tree. A little apple tree—with pink blossoms, and bumblebees buzzing, and sparrows chirping—and fat, low branches he could reach!

Timothy climbed the little tree—holding—pulling—one leg over and up, up, up into the just-right apple tree. He frightened the sparrows, but not the bumblebees. And he smelled the blossoms, and found a nest left over from last year.

Day after day he climbed the little tree, and climbing it was fun.

Then the pink blossoms fell, and tiny green apples grew. Bigger and bigger—little by little—day after day—until they were fat and round and red.

Timothy helped pick them—and eat them.

Then the apples were all gone. The leaves were all gone. The bees buzzed away and didn't come back. But Timothy still climbed the tree, and played in it.

The little tree was Timothy's tree—just the right size for Timothy—day after day.

Until *one* day when the pink blossoms were on it again, and bees buzzing in it, and sparrows chirping, the little tree was TOO SMALL for him! And Timothy was too big! He didn't have to reach. He didn't have to pull. He didn't have to try.

Climbing the little tree was too easy. "And too easy is no fun," said Timothy.

And he remembered the maple tree that was too big when he was too small. Could he climb it? NOW? Maybe he could! So he went to see and he tried it again. He reached up both hands—he stood on tip-toe.

Then he jumped. He grabbed the lowest branch and held on. One leg over and up he went—reaching—pulling—branch after branch. Up climbed Timothy, up the big maple tree!

"I CAN!" cried Timothy. "NOW! because little by little —every day—I've grown bigger and bigger . . . and big enough!"

RASCAL RACCOON AND THE THING CHANGER

BY DAVID BARCLAY

Rascal Raccoon was building something new in the clearing of the woods. It began to look like a big wooden box with electric bulbs and wires in it, and an alarm clock on top. In front there was a big spout and a wide slot opening. At the side there was a small door.

Nobody in the forest trusted Rascal Raccoon because he had been full of mischief since the day he was born. But this box looked so mysterious and exciting that on the evening Rascal wrote directions on it, every animal for miles around crowded in the clearing to see.

On the back of the box Rascal wrote:

THIS MACHINE IS A THING CHANGER.
IT WILL CHANGE ONE THING INTO
THREE THINGS, LIKE ONE APPLE INTO
THREE APPLES. PERSONS USING THE
THING CHANGER MUST THINK RIGHT
OR MACHINE WON'T WORK RIGHT. THE
CHANGER WORKS FROM SIX TO SEVEN
O'CLOCK EVERY NIGHT.

On the door at the side Rascal lettered:

HIGH VOLTAGE — KEEP OUT!

Under the spout in front he wrote:

PUT THING IN HERE,

And under the slot he wrote:

GET THREE THINGS HERE.

All the animals crowded around to read the instructions and study the machine. It was eight o'clock. The machine wouldn't work until the next night. After everyone pressed their ears against the Thing Changer, smelled it, tapped it timidly, they went home to find a thing that they would change into three more things in Rascal Raccoon's machine.

The next evening a line of animals stretched from the Thing Changer all the way into the woods. They all had bags and boxes and strange bundles under their arms. Little Willy Weasel was first in line because he had waited since two o'clock in the afternoon.

The alarm clock went off at exactly six. All the animals cheered and Willy stepped in front of the Changer.

The little weasel shyly unfolded a piece of newspaper and took out a fresh fish that he had just caught. All the animals stood on tip-toe as Willy slid the fish into the spout.

A strange bubbling noise came from the machine. There was a tearing sound, a bell rang, and three little newspaper fish fluttered out of the slot.

Poor Willy picked up the paper fish and walked away.

"Too bad," said Mr. Rabbit. "Willy is too young to think right."

"Too bad," everybody whispered.

"Just wait until it's my turn, Willy, I'll show you how," someone said.

Mr. Rabbit stepped up with a big orange carrot and put it in the spout. The machine bubbled, there was a cracking noise, the bell rang and three little sticks came out the slot.

Everyone laughed. "Not enough practice, Mr. Rabbit!"

Mr. Badger put in a pair of baby badger shoes. He was very poor and two of his children didn't have shoes. The Changer bubbled loudly, the bell rang twice, and the same pair of shoes whisked out the slot.

"The machine only likes food," it was whispered along the line. Many of the animals ran away and came back with new bundles that smelled like food.

But as the creatures dropped in eggs, strawberries or apples, the Thing Changer only tumbled out leaves, twigs, small stones, and scraps of paper. Nobody could think right.

When the last customer, Mr. Box Turtle, had put in a yellow ear of corn, and got three chewed pieces of corn husk back, all the animals started saying, "Where is Rascal Raccoon? Why doesn't he come and show us how to work the Changer?"

Then Mr. Rabbit borrowed Mr. Turtle's pieces of husk, and he showed them to everyone and they all whispered together.

At last Mr. Rabbit said loudly, "Oh, well, let's try again tomorrow." The animals went home.

The next night the line was as long as before and everyone had bundles again. When the alarm clock rang Willy Weasel stepped up and unwrapped a fish, but the fish was four days old and it had a very bad smell. He dropped it into the spout.

The Changer bubbled furiously, and the fish came flying out the slot, but Mr. Rabbit rushed up and dropped in a rotten tomato, and before anything happened Mr. Badger dropped in some spoiled cheese, and everyone dropped in pieces of old food.

The machine bubbled in a rage and stuff came flying out the slot, but then Mr. Bear dropped in a bag of bees, and the bees didn't like being in a bag.

"Ouch!" howled the machine. "Help! Ow! Ouch!" The high voltage door flew open and out popped a very fat Rascal Raccoon, covered with old food and chased by a swarm of angry bees.

"Look!" cried Mr. Rabbit. "Mr. Bear's bees turned into Rascal Raccoon!"

Everyone laughed as Rascal jumped into the pond to get rid of the bees and to wash himself. But the raccoon soon joined the laughter to boast about his clever trick, and he gave the Thing Changer to Mr. Badger to use as a new house.

Everyone agreed that even if Rascal Raccoon was always up to tricks he did liven things up a bit in the forest.

BEDTIME GIGGLES

L. V. FRANCIS

Why is it, when it's time for bed,
The queerest thoughts run through my head?
Each funny bone inside me wiggles,
And makes me get the BEDTIME GIGGLES!

And Mother says, "There's no excuse
For acting like a silly goose!"
I guess my mother's right at that—
I DON'T KNOW WHAT
I'M LAUGHING AT!

THE MAGIC TEAPOT

BY MARY CALHOUN

"I must buy a new teapot," said Mrs. McBobble. Last night she'd dropped and broken her old blue china pot.

So right after breakfast—which didn't taste right without her tea—Mrs. McBobble tied her scarf over her head and hurried off to the store as fast as her little legs would go.

"I'm sorry," said the storekeeper, "but I have only one teapot in the store. I don't know if you'd want it."

From under the counter he brought out a strange-looking teapot with a curlicue handle and a long spout.

"Why, it looks all right," said Mrs. McBobble. "I'll take it."

As soon as she got back home, Mrs. McBobble went right to work in the kitchen to make a pot of tea. When she thought the tea leaves had brewed long enough she poured herself a cup of tea.

But, land of mercy, that wasn't tea in her cup! It looked like—she tasted it—yes, it was hot chocolate!

Poor Mrs. McBobble was all a-fluster. She took the lid off of the teapot and peered inside. But all she saw was amber-colored tea, with black tea leaves floating in it.

So she spilled the hot chocolate into the sink and poured out another cupful. This time her cup was full of lemonade! Well, that was all very well, but Mrs. McBobble wanted *tea*.

Cup after cupful she poured out of the pot, and every time something different came out. Chicken noodle soup, hot and good-smelling. Ice cold root beer. Orange juice with orange ice cubes floating in it.

All this time Mrs. McBobble was getting madder and madder. Her face was red.

"Drat this pot," she said, and dirty dishwater poured out of the teapot, all over the floor.

"Nasty thing," she said, and a mouse jumped out of the teapot's spout.

Mrs. McBobble screamed, for she was afraid of mice. She chased the little gray mouse out of the back door with her broom.

Then she threw the teapot in the trash bin for the garbage man to take away.

But when the garbage man found it, he held it up to look at it.

"Now that's too pretty to throw away," he smiled. And he took it home to his little white house where he lived all alone.

The garbage man didn't like tea, so that night he tried to make coffee in the teapot. He had the same trouble that Mrs. McBobble did. Out came tomato juice.

The garbage man could hardly believe his eyes. He shook the pot and it gurgled. He tried again and got—honey.

Now the garbage man was scowling. He hit the pot a hard jar with his hand, as if to make it work right, and poured another cupful—of castor oil.

"No wonder Mrs. McBobble threw this pot away. There is something very wrong with it," he said angrily.

The next day the garbage man had forgotten about the teapot until he saw his friend, Jennie, a little girl who lived next door. He got the pot from his kitchen and brought it out to Jennie's backyard, where she was playing with her dolls.

"Would you like this old teapot for your doll tea parties?" he asked her.

"Oh yes," Jennie cried, when she saw the gay little teapot. "But don't you need it?"

"It is broken," the garbage man told her. "But it's good enough to play with, isn't it?"

"Yes, thank you," Jennie laughed. "My dolls would love to have some tea."

When the garbage man had gone on to his truck, Jennie set her dolls in a circle around a rock. She brought out her play teacups and saucers and put them around in front of the rag doll, the princess doll, the bride doll and the Indian doll.

Then Jennie took the teapot to the kitchen and ran some water from the faucet into the pot, just to make it real.

"Now we'll have a tea party," she said to the dolls. "Raggedy Ann, would you like some tea?"

Jennie tilted the teapot's spout over the Raggedy Ann doll's cup, and out poured feathers. Lovely white feathers flying about in the breeze.

"Oh!" cried Jennie in delight. "How beautiful! Why, it's a magic teapot." She knew right away.

She poured again and pink lemonade ran out on the ground. She quickly aimed the spout at her cup and caught some lemonade. She tasted it, and it was the best lemonade Jennie had ever drunk.

Jennie filled all the dolls' cups. One teacup had peanuts in it, another cup was full of hot chocolate. The bride doll's cup had fruit punch in it and in the Indian doll's cup was bubble gum.

Jennie wanted some more pink lemonade so she said, "Give me lemonade," and poured into her cup. Instead, out came water.

Jennie was surprised for a minute. She thought hard and then she knew what was wrong.

"I'm sorry, teapot," she said. "PLEASE may I have some lemonade?"

She poured again, and sure enough, out came pink lemonade. Jennie poured and poured all the good things she could think of, and each time she asked the teapot "please" for what she wanted.

It was a magic teapot, so of course, only the magic word "please" made it work right.

LITTLE BUG AND BIG BUG

BY MIRIAM CLARK POTTER

A little bug had a tiny house under a leaf. He had a little blue chair, a little green table, and a little red bed.

One day he went walking up and down a daisy. He had a good time. But when he came home there was a strange bug in his house, a big one with golden eyes.

Little Bug said, "What are you doing here?"

Big Bug said, "The door was open, so I came in. I like your things. Your blue chair is very nice. Your green table looks pretty, and I think I would like to take your little red bed home with me."

"Oh, please don't," said Little Bug. "I like my little red bed."

"But I like it, too. And I can move it so easily; see." Big Bug dragged it across the floor. It made a wee scratchy noise, just like a fingernail on a piece of paper.

"Take my blue chair or my green table," said Little Bug. "But not my little red bed."

"I don't want your blue chair or your green table."

"But what would you do with my red bed?"

"Sleep in it and be cozy."

"But you can't sleep in it!"

"Why not?"

"You are too big for my red bed. Your long black feet would hang over the end."

"I will try it and see," said Big Bug. So he did, and sure enough, his feet did hang over the end, his

long black funny feet. They dangled and kicked.

Little Bug laughed. "Now, you see," he said. "My red bed is the right size for me, but it doesn't fit you. You would not be cozy."

"Well, never mind then," Big Bug told him. "I can sleep on my same old lump of wet mud, or on a slippery-sloppery leaf, or a hot stone, or a cold stick."

"Why, you have lots of beds!" said Little Bug.

"But they aren't as nice as your red bed. Well, good-bye then," said Big Bug.

Little Bug thought his golden eyes looked sad. So he said, "Come some other day, and we will eat two big, fine drops of honey, on my green table. You can sit in my little blue chair."

"But I can't sit in your little blue chair! Don't you remember? Your things don't fit me."

"Well, we'll move my green table out under a lilybell. Then we can sit on pebbles, both of us."

"All right," said Big Bug. Then his golden eyes looked bright. He asked, "Why can't we do that now? Why can't we have a honeydrop party, *immediately?*"

"Oh, all right then," said Little Bug, though he was rather surprised. "We will."

Big Bug helped him move the green table out under the lilybell. Little Bug got two fine drops of honey; a big one for Big Bug, and another one, not quite so big, for himself.

The honey was sweet and sticky and delicious. They ate and talked and laughed.

Then Big Bug said, "Well I must go. Thank you for a *very* nice time."

"Oh, that's all right," said Little Bug. "Come again, some day."

Big Bug went. First he walked, and then he put up his wings and flew. Little Bug watched him.

Then he went walking again, up and down a daisy. He felt very happy. He still had all his things in his house; his blue chair, his green table, and best of all, his little red bed.

And he had a new friend, too!

THE MAGIC PENCIL

BY PEGGY JOHNSON

There was a girl named Linda who was kind. She was kind to her mother, her daddy, and her little brother, Thomas. She was even kind to bugs. When she stepped on an ant on the sidewalk, she always said, "Excuse me." When she found a ladybug on the sidewalk, she always picked it up and put it on her mother's rosebushes.

One day Linda was kind to the toad which lived under her porch. Linda's little brother, Thomas, saw the toad sitting in a puddle.

"Ugh," said Thomas. "You're ugly."

"Don't you know that toads are good?" asked Linda. "They eat mosquitoes, and some toads are elf princes in disguise."

She tucked the toad back under the porch and sent Thomas to fetch it water in a pie tin. The toad winked at Linda and smiled a wide smile.

"Princess," said the toad. (This is the way toads always speak to yellow-haired girls who have just the right number of freckles.) "You helped me. Now I will do something for you. I will give you a penny. Take it to the store and buy a magic pencil." A penny popped out of the toad's mouth.

"What's a magic pencil?" asked Linda.

"It's a drawing pencil," said the toad. "You draw a picture with it, then clap your hands three times and the picture will come to life."

"What does a magic pencil look like?"

"You'll know when you see it," replied the toad.

Sure enough, when Linda arrived at the store and looked into the box of penny pencils on the counter, she knew. There were two red pencils, two yellow pencils, two brown pencils, but only one blue pencil. Linda decided that the blue one was the magic pencil.

She took it home and put it on her bedside table. That night when everything was quiet so she could think, she thought about what she would like to have first.

In less than a minute she knew. Linda sat up in bed. She put her book on her knees, and drew a horse. It was the best horse she had ever drawn. It had eyes like stars and a tail like a broom. When it was finished, Linda clapped her hands three times.

There was a horse sitting on her lap.

Luckily the horse was small, so Linda was not hurt. She was just uncomfortable and had to call her daddy to take the horse off the bed. He led the horse outside and tied it to an apple tree. Linda found it in the morning eating apples, and she rode all morning.

But that afternoon it rained. She had to stay in the house with Thomas. He cried about the rain.

"I wanted to go to the zoo today," sobbed Thomas.

"Don't cry," said Linda. "I will draw a zoo animal for you."

They sat at the kitchen table with paper in front of them, and Linda drew an elephant. It had wrinkled knees and three hairs on the end of its tail. Linda was careful to leave the paper on the table and not on her lap. She clapped her hands three times.

There was an elephant standing on the table. He was too heavy for the table and he mashed it flat. He was too fat to walk through the kitchen door. Linda's daddy had to cut a big hole in the wall to let the elephant out. They gave the elephant to the zoo, and the zoo was happy to have the only elephant in the world with three hairs in its tail.

The next day was Linda's daddy's birthday. Linda thought she would give her daddy a nice new car, so she drew one. She had trouble drawing the circles for the wheels. They looked like building blocks. Then she took the picture of the car out in the yard and clapped her hands.

There stood a beautiful car. Her daddy was SO pleased. He couldn't drive the new car, however, because it had square wheels. He had to save his money to buy a set of round ones.

For weeks Linda's daddy was so busy saving money he forgot to give Linda her allowance, and so she could not buy any candy. She was so hungry for candy that she drew a whole page of pictures of her favorite kinds. There were peppermint canes and licorice sticks and lollypops and those orange peanuts that taste like bananas. There was a huge pile of candy in front of her, and she ate it all.

Of course she had a stomach ache, and the doctor was called.

"It is probably only a stomach ache," he said, "but it might be the Pip. I'll give her a shot."

Linda hated shots, so while the doctor was looking in his bag for his needle, she drew a doll. The doll had yellow hair and a few freckles. It looked like Linda.

Linda tucked the doll's picture under her blanket, then quickly slipped down under the bed. She clapped her hands three times, and there was a big doll lying in her bed!

The doctor gave it a shot.

"My, you're strong," said the doctor. "You bent my needle, but you didn't cry a bit. Here's something for being brave." He left a dime on the bedside table.

Linda used the dime to buy drawing paper, on which she drew things for the new doll. She drew pretty dresses and all kinds of clothes. Then she drew a house for her doll with an upstairs and a downstairs. It even had a patio with a big fish pond. And finally, she drew furniture for every room. She drew so many things that the magic pencil was worn down to a little stub, no longer than Linda's thumb. She took the big pile of pictures and clapped her hands three times.

There stood a doll house, big enough for a girl to walk inside. It had lights that really lit and a stove that really cooked, and there was a pile of furniture and doll clothes on the roof. Thomas brought a stepladder and helped Linda carry the things down.

"Let's have a party," Linda said. "I'll bake cookies on the doll's stove, and you set the table. Put something pretty in the middle."

Linda thought Thomas would pick some flowers, so she was surprised when she saw a dish of marbles on the table.

"Where did you get those pretty marbles, Thomas?" she asked.

"Daddy gave them to me today for my birthday," said Thomas. "I wanted a dog, but Daddy is saving his money for wheels so he could only buy marbles."

Linda felt sorry she had forgotten her brother's birthday.

"I'll draw a birthday dog for you."

They stretched out on the floor of the doll house, and Linda began to draw with her little stub of magic pencil.

"What kind of tail do you want on this dog?" she asked.

"Long," answered Thomas.

Linda drew a long tail. "What kind of ears?"

"Long," said Thomas.

Linda drew long spaniel ears. "What else?" she asked.

"A spot," said Thomas.

Linda started to draw a spot, but right in the middle of the spot she came to the end of the magic pencil. She finished drawing the spot with an ordinary pencil. She clapped her hands.

There was a dog with long ears and a long tail dancing around Thomas. It bounced up to lick his cheek. Thomas patted it and half of the black spot on its back rubbed off, so instead of naming the dog Spot, Thomas named it Half Spot.

Now the magic pencil was gone, but Linda was happy. Her brother had a dog. Her daddy had a car, and one day he saved enough money to buy wheels and he took the whole family for a ride to the zoo to see the elephant. And Linda had a horse and a new doll and a doll house.

What more could a little girl want?

MARTIN THE MAGPIE

BY LOIS WATSON

Do you know what a magpie is?

Is it a rug for wiping your feet?

Is it a new dessert with whipped cream on top?

Is it a dance?

Is it a bird?

It *is* a bird! The magpie is a bird with a long, long tail. And he chatters, chatters all day long—"Cheek-cheek-cheek-ma-a-a-g!"

And if you'll be very, very quiet, I'll tell you the story of Martin the Magpie and how he found the Silence.

Martin was just about the talkingest magpie you or I might ever see. He talked more than you do. He talked more than I do.

He talked to the squirrels as they looked for nuts. He talked to the ants while they built their ant hills. He talked to the leaves as they danced in the wind. He talked to the bees and the butterflies and the beetles. And when he couldn't find anyone to talk to, he talked to himself. All day long he chattered, chattered, chattered.

One spring day, Martin was sitting high up in a pine tree. In that same tree, Mother Dove was putting her babies to sleep, singing to them with her soft "Coooooo." But every time the little doves closed their eyes, Martin would shout, "Cheek-cheek-cheek-ma-a-a-g!" and wake them up.

Mother Dove finally called up to Martin, "Can we have a little silence, please!"

"Silence?" said Martin. "Why of course! I'll get you some Silence." But Martin didn't know what Silence was because he'd never learned about Silence. Still, he wanted to be helpful, so he called back, "I'll get you some Silence, Mother Dove," and away he flew.

First he flew to the squirrels who were counting their nuts left over from winter storage. "Forty-one,

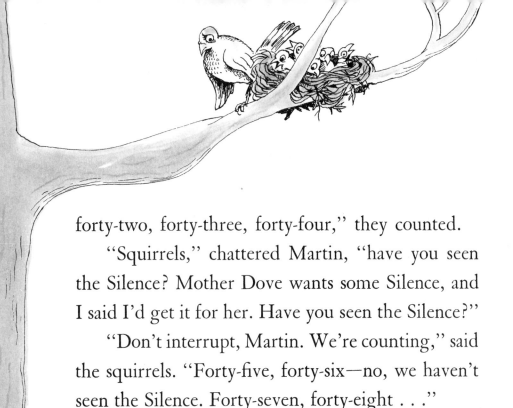

forty-two, forty-three, forty-four," they counted.

"Squirrels," chattered Martin, "have you seen the Silence? Mother Dove wants some Silence, and I said I'd get it for her. Have you seen the Silence?"

"Don't interrupt, Martin. We're counting," said the squirrels. "Forty-five, forty-six—no, we haven't seen the Silence. Forty-seven, forty-eight . . ."

"Too bad, too bad, cheek-cheek-cheek-ma-a-a-g!" cried Martin, and he flew to the brook.

"Brook," called Martin, "have you seen the Silence? Mother Dove wants the Silence, and I said I'd get it for her. Have you seen the Silence?"

"Bubble, bubble, bibble, bubble, splash," said the brook. "Don't trouble me with foolish questions. Bubble and splash is all I know. Bubble, bubble, babble, bubble, bibble, bubble, splash."

"Oh dear," said Martin. "Cheek-cheek-cheek-ma-a-ag! Where can it be?" and he flew to the bees.

The bees were hard at work gathering nectar from the spring flowers for honey. "Buzz-z-z, bizz-z-z, what a lovely flower this is-z-z-z," they said.

"Bees," called Martin, "have you seen the Silence? I've been looking all over for the Silence, because Mother Dove wants some Silence, and I said I'd get it for her. Have you seen the Silence?"

But the bees just answered, "Never was-z-z anything but Buzz-z-z. We don't know what the Silence is-z-z. All we know is busy, buzz, and honey."

"Goodness," said Martin. "Maybe there isn't any Silence around here. Now, who can tell me where to find it?"

And then he thought of Old Owl who lived deep in the woods. And he flew to the Old Owl's house, chattering all the way.

Old Owl was sitting in a large oak tree, and when Martin saw him, he called to him, "Old Owl, can you help me? I'm looking for the Silence, and I don't know how to find it."

And do you know what Old Owl did?

First, he laughed three times, "Hoo, hoo, hoo." Then he blinked his eyes once and said, "Ssh! Listen!"

For the first time in his life, Martin stopped talking and listened. It was very, very quiet deep in the forest. There wasn't a sound.

"I don't hear anything," whispered Martin.

"Good," said Old Owl.

"Is this where I look for the Silence?" whispered Martin. "I don't see anything."

"You don't *see* Silence, Martin," said Old Owl. You *hear* it. Or rather, it's what you *don't* hear."

"But I don't hear anything," said Martin again, and again he listened. As he listened, he started to think. Then he said softly, "You mean *this* is Silence? When everything is quiet?"

Old Owl blinked twice and nodded.

"You mean, when the bees stop buzzing and the squirrels stop chattering and—and I stop talking? That's Silence?"

Old Owl blinked three times and nodded.

"Oh," said Martin. He listened again. "You know," he said, "it's not bad. I like it. It's very soothing. Thank you, Old Owl. I'll go back to Mother Dove and show her that now I know what Silence is."

Martin flew quietly away, back to the pine tree. It was evening by this time, and the Dove babies were fast asleep. Martin hopped out on the branch above them and looked down at them and smiled.

MOTHER'S LITTLE HELPER

PEGGY JOHNSON

I helped my mother
make the bed.
"Why, what's that lump?"
my mother said,
And she was so surprised
to see
The lump in bed was
only ME!

THE LLAMAS' PAJAMAS

BY CLAUDINE WIRTHS

Once there were two little llamas named Yama
Llama and Bahama Llama. And of course there was
Mama Llama.

Now Bahama Llama and Yama Llama were
rather good little llamas, but they were careless about
one thing—hanging up their pajamas. Every morning Mama Llama would say, "Did you hang up your
pajamas, little llamas? Something might happen to
them if you don't."

"Yes, Mama Llama," Bahama Llama and Yama Llama would reply. "We hung up our pajamas."

But sometimes even when they said they did, they didn't!

For goodness sakes, what could happen to your pajamas even if you did leave them on the floor?

One fine morning Mama Llama called Yama and Bahama. "Quick, quick, little llamas, get out of bed. Your Aunt Hominy Llama and your cousins Ali and Bama are going to meet us downtown at the Cyclorama. If you hurry we can just make the nine o'clock bus to town. Dress in your very best, little llamas. And don't forget to hang up your pajamas!"

My, how they scampered! Yama Llama jumped out of her bed, threw off her red pajamas and skipped into her clothes. Bahama Llama jumped out of her bed, snatched off her green pajamas and scrambled into her clothes. And then they raced to catch up with Mama Llama who was already waiting at the door. They never gave another thought to the green and red pajamas they left lying on the floor.

Well, Mama, Yama, and Bahama Llama had barely caught the bus for town when Mrs. Brown Mouse (who lived in the kitchen of the Llama house) came tip-tip-tipping out of her hole. The last time the Llamas went away she had seen just what she wanted. Would it still be there today?

Mrs. Brown Mouse went all over the house. First she looked in the kitchen, but she didn't see it there. "Eeenh, eeenh, eeenh!" she squeaked crossly.

Next she looked all over the living room. But did she find what she was looking for? "Eenh, eeenh, eeenh!"

And then she tried the bathroom. "Eeenh, eeenh, eeenh!" She just couldn't remember where she had seen it before.

Suddenly she remembered! Down the hall she scooted straight to Bahama's and Yama's room. "EEEEEEEEEE!" she squeaked in delight. Just inside the room on the floor (just where it was before) she saw just what she wanted. Can you guess what it was? It was a pile of llamas' pajamas.

Tip-tip-tippy she marched off down the hall dragging Yama's red pajamas behind her right across the kitchen floor and into the hole in the kitchen wall. Back she came in a moment and dragged Bahama's green pajamas tip-tip-tippy down the hall and through the hole in the wall.

It was late that night when Bahama Llama, Yama Llama, and Mama Llama returned from town. They had seen every single inch of the Cyclorama and had shopped all over town. Mama Llama bought a new hat, Bahama Llama bought a jump rope, and Yama had a wind-up cat. They had even bought two little brown gowns to give to their cousins Ali and Bama when their birthdays came around. My, but they were tired.

So tired that Mama Llama said, "Come, little llamas, go get your pajamas. It's high time you were both in bed." Well, Yama Llama yawned and Bahama Llama yawned and went straight-away to their room. But when they got there, they couldn't find their pajamas anywhere.

They looked under their beds (where they sometimes kicked them). They looked on the chairs (where they sometimes dropped them), and even in the cabinets (where they sometimes flopped them with their toys). But the llamas' pajamas were nowhere to be found.

"Oh for goodness sakes," said Mama Llama. "They didn't just get up and walk away by themselves. Look around!"

The two little llamas looked all over the house, but all they found was a little lady mouse who giggled and squeaked as they passed her house.

After all that searching and the day in town the two little llamas were so tired and cross. They went into the kitchen to Mama Llama and flopped out on the floor. Bahama had just closed one eye when she heard Yama cry, "Look, Mama Llama, I can see my pajamas in the mouse hole."

All three llamas took turns putting their eyes to the hole. There was the snuggest, warmest nest made up of red and green pajamas. And in the nest

were four little furry bright-eyed mice!

"We want our pajamas!" cried Yama and Bahama. "Mama, make them give us back our pajamas. They're just made for little llamas—not for mice!"

But proud Mrs. Mouse just looked at the red and green nest that looked so nice in her house. And four little furry heads shook back and forth. "Eeenh, eenh, eenh!" they said.

Sadly, Yama and Bahama looked at their mama. Then getting to their feet they waved good-bye to their lovely pajamas.

It was a sad night for the two little llamas when they lost their pajamas because they had to go to bed in the silly brown gowns of their cousins.

And from that day to this you can bet your best nightgown you'll find no pajamas on the floors of Bahama and Yama Llama.